For Maia

OXFORD
UNIVERSITY PRESS

Great Clarendon Street, Oxford OX2 6DP

Oxford University Press is a department of the University of Oxford.
It furthers the University's objective of excellence in research, scholarship,
and education by publishing worldwide in

Oxford New York

Athens Auckland Bangkok Bogotá Buenos Aires
Cape Town Chennai Dar es Salaam Delhi Florence Hong Kong Istanbul
Karachi Kolkata Kuala Lumpur Madrid Melbourne Mexico City Mumbai
Nairobi Paris São Paulo Shanghai Singapore Taipei Tokyo Toronto Warsaw

with associated companies in Berlin Ibadan

Oxford is a registered trade mark of Oxford University Press
in the UK and in certain other countries

British Library Cataloguing in Publication Data available

Hardback ISBN 0-19-910670-3
Paperback ISBN 0-19-910671-1

1 3 5 7 9 10 8 6 4 2

Printed in Italy

Benedict Blathwayt

In the
Town

OXFORD
UNIVERSITY PRESS

This is where we live

road

footpath

subway

tunnel

flyover

pavement

bridge

lamp-post

runway

reservoir

flats

steps

We are going shopping

bus stop

supermarket

garden centre

toilets

shopping trolley

garage

car park

shopping basket

petrol pump

cattle market

snack bar

delivery lorry

We are going on a journey

 ticket

 loudspeaker

 timetable

 clock

 luggage trolley

 map

 suitcase

 ticket machine

 backpack

 ticket office

 guard

 telephone

How we get around

bicycle

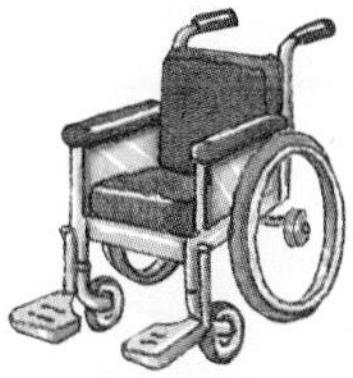

wheelchair

taxi

truck

train

balloon

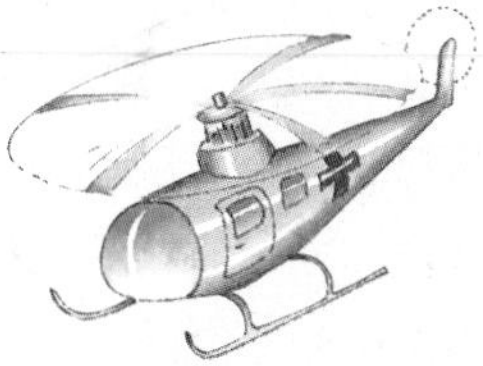

motorbike

helicopter

boat

bus

car

aeroplane

Playing in the park

ball

litterbin

skates

swings

flower bed

pushchair

sandpit

skateboard

bench

pond

slide

tree

Our town centre

cinema

fire station

hospital

museum

restaurant

theatre

toyshop

bandstand

post office

library

church

police station

market

bank

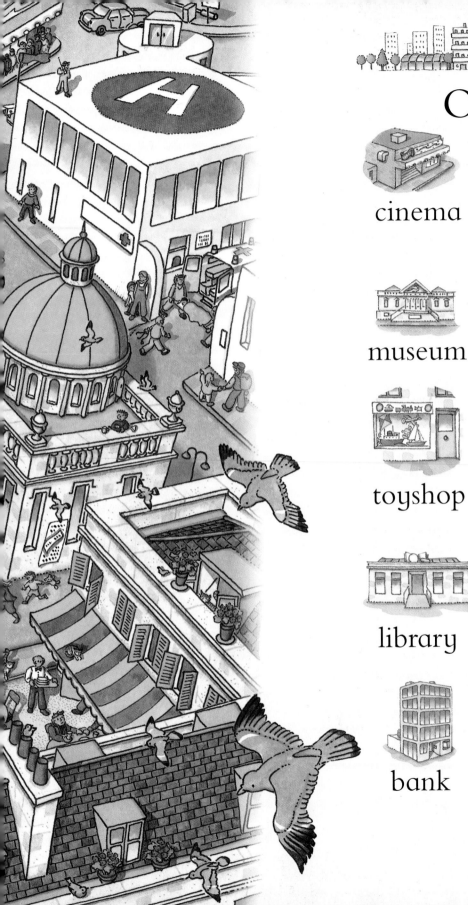

17

Market day

stall

money

list

purse

cakes

shellfish

flowers

fish

toys

fruit

bread

vegetables

sparrows

boxes

19

Loading and unloading

crane

container

crate

conveyor

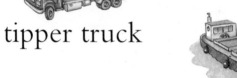
tipper truck

skip lorry

grain silo

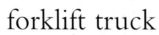
forklift truck

barge

ship

storage tank

fuel tanker

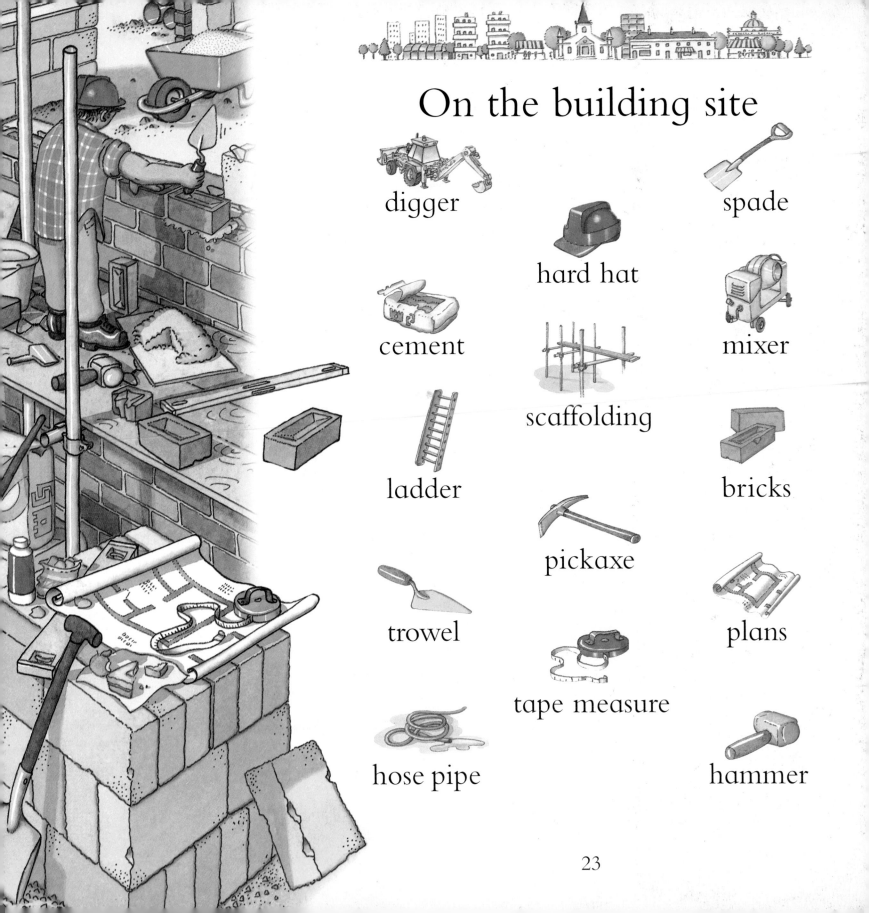

On the building site

digger

spade

hard hat

cement

mixer

scaffolding

ladder

bricks

pickaxe

trowel

plans

tape measure

hose pipe

hammer

23

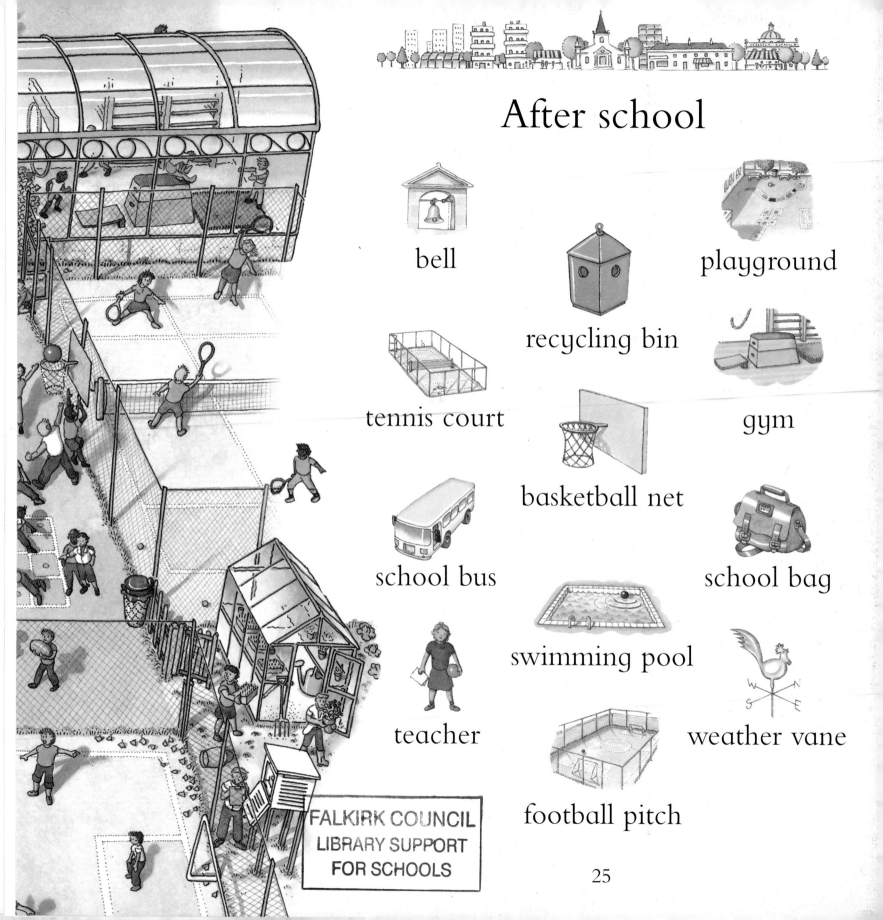

After school

bell

recycling bin

playground

tennis court

gym

basketball net

school bus

school bag

teacher

swimming pool

weather vane

football pitch

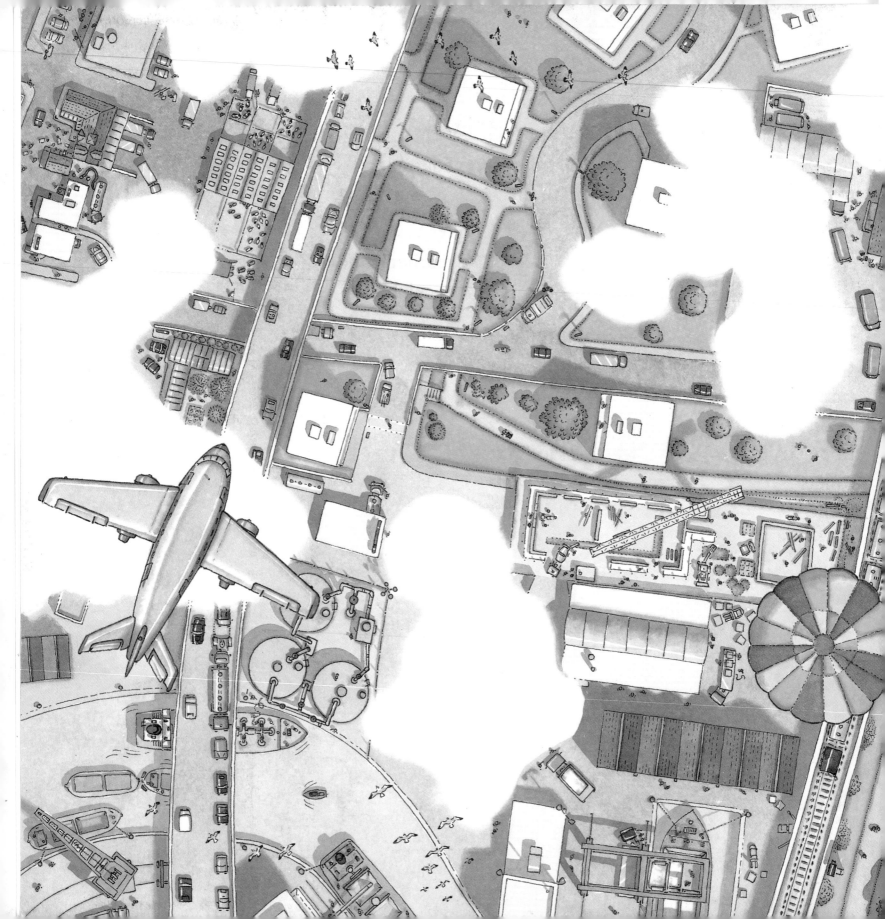

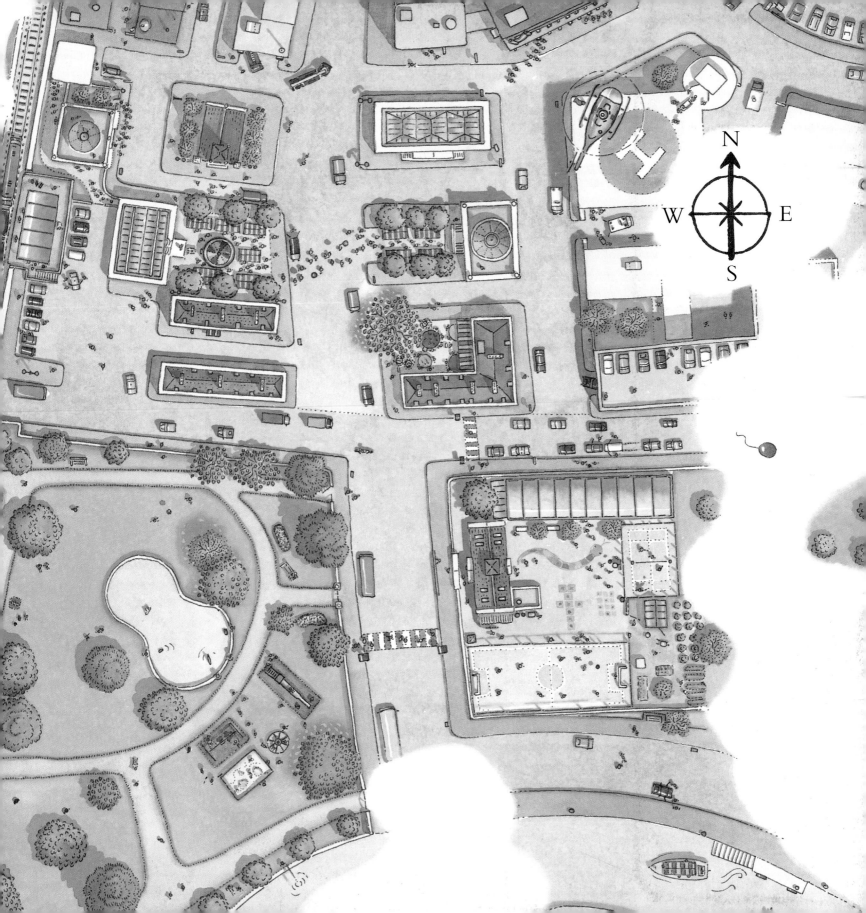